Glamour! ✳ Talent!

✳ Stardom! ✳

✳ Fame and fortune ✳
could be one step away!

Welcome to

Fame School

For another fix of

read
Reach for the Stars
Rising Star
Secret Ambition
Rivals!
Tara's Triumph
Lucky Break
Solo Star
Pop Diva
Battle of the Bands
Star Maker
Dancing Star
Summer Spectacular

Fame School

Christmas Stars

Cindy Jefferies

USBORNE

I would like to dedicate this book with much love
to the memory of Mike and Lilias Jefferies.
They were the very best of parents and I owe them everything.

First published in 2006 by Usborne Publishing Ltd., Usborne House,
83-85 Saffron Hill, London EC1N 8RT, England. www.usborne.com

A CIP catalogue record for this book is available from the British Library.

JFMAMJJA OND/09 94359

ISBN 9780746077429

Printed in Yeovil, Somerset, UK.

 1 A New Idea

"Look at this!" Pop was staring at a notice that had been pinned up outside the dining room at Rockley Park School. Pop didn't usually read the notices, especially since she and her friends had all gone up a year. It was different when they had been new. Then, *everything* had been exciting. By now, Pop knew that notices were often about boring things like lost property. But this brightly coloured one had really caught her eye.

"What is it?" asked Chloe, who shared a room with Pop and her twin sister Lolly.

"It's about the Christmas Concert," said Pop, sounding very excited. "Wow!"

Christmas Stars

Christmas was always a fun time, although there were numerous performances of one kind or another at the school every term. Rockley Park was *the* place for students to learn all there was to know about making it in the music business. Everyone at the school wanted to be a star and the school gave them lots of opportunities to perform. Chloe couldn't help wondering what had got Pop so excited about this one. She and Lolly joined Pop at the noticeboard to have a look.

Christmas Concert Challenge! said the notice. *Instead of the usual Christmas Concert, I'd like to see each class come up with a Christmas theme to link their performances around. Let's have some coordination, fun and a real festive feel. Please get your ideas to me by the end of the week. I will award a prize for the theme I enjoy most!* It was signed *Judge Jim Henson.*

"It does sound a bit different," said Chloe. "Trust Judge Jim to come up with a new idea!"

"It doesn't give us long," said Lolly. She sounded

rather concerned. "And what exactly does he mean? How many themes does he want for the concert?"

"There's plenty of time," said Pop. "And it's obvious. Look!" She jabbed her finger at the notice. "Each class has to think of a different theme. I bet I can easily think of loads to choose from. And there's a prize for the best one! I wonder what the prize will be..." She nudged her sister. "I bet we could win if we put our minds to it. Let's give it a go!" Pop looked at Chloe and grinned. "Our whole class has a singing lesson next," she said. "Mr. Player won't mind if we discuss the concert. I bet we'll have it all sorted by the end of the day."

"What sort of theme do you think we should have, then?" asked Chloe. "I can't think of anything right now."

"Honestly, you two!" said Pop, rolling her eyes in mock despair. "How about something like *The Twelve Days of Christmas*, or...*Jingle Bells*...or maybe a bit from a pantomime like *Cinderella*? You could sing something as Cinderella, Chloe, and Lolly and I could do an ugly sisters' duet."

Christmas Stars

Chloe burst out laughing. Pop and Lolly Lowther were already famous models – and had been since they were tiny. With their amazing looks, it would be crazy to cast *them* as ugly sisters! All the same, Pop had fired up Chloe's enthusiasm. Maybe a themed concert *would* be fun.

It was obvious as soon as they arrived at Mr. Player's room that lots of the other students had seen the notice as well.

"What do you think of Judge Jim's idea?" Ed, who was an enthusiastic guitarist, asked the girls. "I don't like it at all. I just want to play my guitar, not dress up. After all, we're not in a theatre school, are we? I won't get any Rising Stars points if I have to act!"

The Christmas Concert had always followed the format of every other concert on the school calendar. Each pupil simply performed a song, a piece of music or a dance routine they had prepared during the term. They were assessed on their performances, and awarded Rising Stars points, so concerts weren't simply about having fun. The pupils who had earned the most points during the year got to perform in the special Rising Stars Concert on regional television, so it was no wonder that every performance was taken seriously.

"It doesn't mean acting, does it?" asked Tara Fitzgerald, the girls' other roommate. "If it does, I'm not having anything to do with it." She folded her arms and looked stubborn.

"I wouldn't mind!" said Marmalade, grinning from ear to ear. His wild, ginger hair had won him the crazy nickname that suited him so well. He was a very talented dancer and also tended to be the class clown. "Perhaps I could do the dance of the Sugar Plum Fairy in big clumpy boots. Do you think that would win the prize?"

"I doubt it." Pop laughed. "That's hardly a theme, is it? But it would be very funny."

"The notice didn't say anything about acting," Chloe pointed out. "I think Judge Jim is just trying to make the Christmas Concert a bit more interesting."

"Well said, Chloe!" Mr. Player came into the room

and smiled. "It sounds as if you've got the right idea. Have all of you seen the notice?" he asked the class. Most of the students nodded.

"But how do we choose a theme to suit us all?" said Danny James, one of Marmalade's roommates and his best friend.

"I don't think it really matters," said Mr. Player. "You just need to choose something you like and fit all your performances to it. Has anyone had any ideas yet?"

"I wondered about *The Twelve Days of Christmas*," said Pop.

"But we've only got two drummers," Tara objected.

Pop scowled at her.

"What about something more general and wintry like snow?" said Ben.

"Too boring," pronounced Tara.

"Well, you think of something then!" said Marmalade.

"I don't want to do it anyway," said Tara. "I'm a musician, not a comic turn."

"Oh, I don't know about that," said Marmalade with a slow grin.

A New Idea

"Come on, now," Mr. Player said quickly, before Tara could explode at Marmalade's teasing. "The idea behind this is to get you to work together, not fall out. Let's have some more thoughts."

"Pop mentioned using a scene from a pantomime," said Chloe.

"Yeah!" said Ed. "That's a good idea. Ugly sisters! Ben and I could do that!" Ed and Ben were Marmalade's other two roommates and did everything together.

"Cool!" agreed Ben. "I fancy being an ugly-sister rock guitarist!"

"We saw *Beauty and the Beast* last Christmas," said Lolly. "That's a good pantomime as well."

"I like *Jack and the Beanstalk* best," said Danny.

As she listened, an idea started to come to Chloe. "We don't have time to do a whole pantomime," she told everyone. "And we all have different favourites anyway, so it would be difficult to choose one. Maybe we could pretend we're in a new pantomime that brings all the traditional characters together."

"Yes!" agreed Marmalade. "And how about if we're rehearsing and have seen a poster somewhere for a concert at Rockley Park?"

"And we wish we were musically talented like the people there!" added Chloe with a laugh.

"Brilliant!" said Lolly. "There's often magic in pantomimes and that means our wishes can come true. Each pantomime character could make a wish and then find they really can create music."

"Great!" said Ben.

"That's a really clever idea," said Mr. Player. "And you got to it with teamwork. Well done! Now, if you don't mind, I think we ought to get on with the lesson. You can develop your theme over lunch if you like, but now it's time for some singing!"

2 An Important Meeting

There were a few more lessons to get through before lunch, but as soon as maths was over everyone hurried to the dining room. Several other groups of students had already arrived and there was a lot of organizing going on.

"Let's get things sorted out," suggested Pop. "We need a couple more chairs and someone ought to queue up for food."

"I'll do food," offered Chloe.

"I'll come with you," said Lolly.

"I'll help carry as well," said Danny. "What does everyone want to eat?"

"Just get a selection of rolls and some salad," said

Pop. "It'll be quicker that way and I'm sure we'll all find something we like."

After they had eaten, everyone wanted to speak at the same time and the discussion was rather chaotic. But Pop soon put a stop to that. "We need to be more organized or we'll never get anything done," she complained. "We need someone in charge."

"You're a good organizer, Pop," said Chloe. "Why don't *you* be in charge?"

Pop looked doubtful. "It's no good someone trying to take over if everyone else doesn't agree," she said.

"Well, why don't we vote on it?" said Ben.

"Good idea," agreed Marmalade. "Does anyone else want to be the organizer?"

There were a few mutterings from Charlie Owen's direction, but no one actually put themselves forward.

"Okay," said Marmalade. "Let's have a show of hands, then. Who is happy to have Pop in charge?"

Most people put their hands up straight away. Tara shrugged, but she raised her hand too.

"Is that everyone?" asked Chloe. She looked at

Charlie, who slowly raised his hand as well. "It looks as if you're it," Chloe told Pop. "Good luck!"

Pop looked pleased. "Thanks," she said. "Why don't we all have a think about which characters we'd like to be and I'll make a list? That would be a good start."

"Ugly sisters!" yelled Ed and Ben together.

"Dick Whittington," said Marmalade. "I'll get my little sister to post me her toy cat."

"You ought to be Beauty," Chloe suggested to Lolly.

"Yeah!" agreed several people and Lolly blushed.

"What about you, Pop?" Chloe asked.

Pop was busy scribbling names and characters down on a piece of paper as they were shouted out. "Oh, I think I'll just be something like the pantomime producer," she said.

"The characters could be a rather hopeless group of actors." Ed laughed. "After all, none of us *can* really act, can we?"

"That's a good idea," agreed Pop, scribbling hard. "What do you think?" she asked the whole group.

"I think you ought to dress up as Judge Jim," said

Tara. "With a clipboard and a harassed expression, while trying to stay laid-back."

Chloe stared at Tara. She wasn't sure if the idea was a serious one or not, but the thought of dressing Pop up as the popular, dreadlocked, elderly head of the Rock Department was a brilliant one. He organized all the concerts and Tara was right, he did work very hard but always seemed laid-back too. Chloe thought Pop would look really funny dressed as him.

"If you want to have someone dressed up as Judge Jim, wouldn't it be better to choose a boy?" asked Pop doubtfully.

"No way!" several people shouted out.

"It'll be hysterical if you do it," Ed said. "And he'll love it. He's got a good sense of humour. Great idea, Tara!"

"I'm not turning my hair into dreads!" Pop told them, clutching her sleek hair in mock horror.

"Don't worry," said Lolly. "We can just plait it for you."

"And add some talcum powder to make it grey," suggested Danny.

Pop didn't look too impressed at this. But then

she giggled. "I'll look ridiculous!" she said.

"That's the point!" Chloe told her enthusiastically. "I bet our bit of the concert will be by far the best. We'll show everyone that we can be funny as well as serious artists."

"What about your character?" Pop asked Chloe. "Have you decided what you want to be?"

"I'm not sure," said Chloe.

"Well, we don't have a Cinderella yet," said Pop, running her finger down the list. "I've got a cool dress I could lend you for that. It's white with sequins, and you could borrow my sparkly silver shoes."

"Okay!" said Chloe. She'd seen the dress in Pop's wardrobe and it was seriously cool. She'd feel brilliant wearing it. "Thanks a lot! What about you, Tara?" she added.

Tara shrugged. "I'm not into all this dressing-up stuff," she said.

"But you must!" said Marmalade. "You can't be the only one not to join in!"

"Well...I suppose I wouldn't mind being Snow

White's wicked stepmother," she told him.

"But she's a horrible character," protested Lolly.

"So are the ugly sisters," pointed out Tara. "Besides, she gets to wear black and purple, so I've got most of my costume already."

"Fair enough," said Pop, glancing at Tara's clothes. "I suppose you do always wear black." She wrote down Tara's character and drew a line underneath. "I think we've done everything we can right now," she added. "We all need to go away and sort out costumes and decide on our individual musical performances. They are still the most important part of the concert. Once everyone knows what they're doing, we'll have another meeting and put the acts in order, with little linking bits to join them together. Has anyone got anything else to say before we finish the meeting?"

"I've got a suggestion," said Ben. "I know we have to tell Judge Jim what our theme is but why don't we keep Pop's character a secret? That way it'll be a real surprise for him!"

"Brilliant!" agreed Ed. "He'll love that."

"Are you sure he won't be annoyed?" asked Lolly.

"Of course not!" said Charlie. "He loves a laugh."

"Okay," agreed Pop. "We won't tell him. How about another meeting soon? We mustn't waste time."

Everyone seemed to think that was a good idea and the meeting broke up. Chloe helped put the tables back where they belonged. "This concert is going to be great fun, isn't it?" she said to Lolly.

"Yes," agreed Lolly. "As long as Pop doesn't get too carried away with being in charge!"

"I expect she'll be okay," Chloe told her. "Don't worry. She'll soon get shouted at if she gets too big for her boots."

"Oh!" Lolly put her hands up to her face. "I've just had a terrible thought!"

Chloe looked at her anxiously. "What's the matter?" she asked.

"Well, you know how Pop and I always sing together?" Lolly told Chloe.

"Yes. Of course." Pop 'n' Lolly were planning on breaking into the pop-music business, just as they had into modelling, by using the fact that they were glamorous, identical twins, so they always sang as a double act.

"Well, how are we going to be able to perform together at the concert with me dressed as Beauty and Pop as Judge Jim?"

Chloe stared at her friend and then started to giggle. "You'll be more like Beauty and the Beast than Pop 'n' Lolly." She laughed.

"It's not funny, Chloe," said Lolly. "You know very well how important every concert is. We'll still be marked on our performances, even if this is going to be a different sort of production. Anyway," she added, "Judge Jim isn't anything like a beast."

Chloe tried very hard to stop herself from laughing about Pop trying to be part of Pop 'n' Lolly while still dressed as Judge Jim. "I know he isn't," she agreed. "And don't worry. I'm sure Mr. Player will help you choose an appropriate song." She gave Lolly a hug. "Actually, I'll bet once you start to sing, your professionalism will carry you through," she added more seriously. "Music is much more important to all of us than any silly clothes we might be wearing."

"I just hope our teachers can see that too," fretted Lolly.

"Of course they will," Chloe reassured her. "They know how seriously Pop takes her career and after all it'll be her wearing the silly clothes."

"That's true," agreed Lolly, looking a lot happier.

"Besides," added Chloe. "Maybe Pop could do a quick change before your song. Whatever happens, I'm sure you'll be fine. And I think it's going to be the best concert ever!"

3 A Tired Teacher

After school, Chloe and Lolly went with Pop to tell Judge Jim about their class's idea for a Christmas theme. As they were all pop singers, none of the girls had lessons with the head of the Rock Department. But because Judge Jim always ran the main school concerts, they knew him quite well. He was Chloe's favourite member of staff because he had found her in floods of tears on her audition day and had been wonderful at calming her down and sorting her out.

The girls found Judge Jim in his office, struggling with the mountain of paperwork that was always piled up on his desk and the floor. Normally, he had some blues playing quietly while he worked, but today the

CD player was silent. Chloe noticed straight away how tired he looked.

"Come in, girls. Come in," he welcomed them. "What are you wantin'?" he asked, passing his hand wearily over his face. "You come to offer me some help with all this?" He waved his hand over the papers and smiled slightly.

"Actually, we came to tell you about our theme for the concert," said Pop.

"Good!" he said approvingly. "You're the first. So, come on. Tell me what you're thinkin'."

Pop explained their idea of dressing up as pantomime characters who wished they could be talented singers and musicians. "The characters will be discussing the Rockley Park acts they've seen described on a poster," she told him. "So for instance, Chloe's character, Cinderella, might say something like *I wish I could sing like Chloe Tompkins!* Then she'll sing her song to the others. We were hoping that would be good enough to pull all our acts together."

"Sounds good to me," he told them. "Clever, too!

It means you can choose whatever you like to perform, because your characters provide the theme rather than the music. I wondered how students might cope with having to give all their acts the same theme, but you've neatly got round that problem!"

"Thank you!" said Chloe and Pop together.

"I'll look forward to seeing the links between each act," Judge Jim said. "You should be able to have some fun with them."

"We think so, too!" said Pop, grinning broadly. Lolly gave her sister a subtle nudge, but Pop just grinned even more. "Can you tell us what the prize will be?" she asked him.

"I thought I'd take the class with the most enjoyable theme out for a pizza next term," he told her.

"That sounds fun!" said Chloe.

"It's just as well we're a small school," said Pop. "If we had large classes, a prize like that would cost a fortune!"

"Yes." Judge Jim nodded and looked at the pile of papers on his desk. "I'd better get on," he muttered. "Thank you for coming so promptly," he told the girls. "I approve of your idea and I'll make a note of it. Now if you'll excuse me…"

He glanced at the heap of papers again and Chloe took the hint. "Yes. We must go," she said quickly.

As soon as they were out of the Rock Department, Pop punched the air in triumph. "The first to go and see him!" she crowed. "Our section of the concert is going to be *so* cool. We're going to beat everyone else. Just you wait and see!"

"I was afraid you were going to let on about your role," said Lolly.

"No way!" said Pop. "That's our secret weapon."

"Did you think Judge Jim looked tired?" asked Chloe, as they made their way back to their room to relax before tea.

"A bit, I suppose," agreed Lolly.

"I thought he looked *terribly* tired," Chloe insisted. "He must be as old as my grandfather, but Grandpa is retired and Judge Jim has *heaps* of work to do all the time. I hope he's okay."

"I'm sure he is," said Lolly reassuringly.

"He's used to it," Pop added airily. "Someone like Judge Jim simply *lives* for music and this school."

The girls reached their door and Pop flung it open with a flourish as she so often did. It crashed against a cupboard with a loud bang and she grinned. "Someone like him," she continued, taking no notice of Tara's scowl from across the room, "he'll go on for ever."

"I wish you wouldn't do that," Tara objected, looking pointedly at the door. "And who will go on for ever?"

Pop closed the door with an elaborately gentle click and sat on her bed. "Judge Jim," she explained. "We've just been to see him and Chloe thought he was looking tired but I said—"

"He *is* tired," Tara interrupted. She knew Judge Jim better than the other girls because she was a rock musician and had lessons with him. "He told us the other day that he's always exhausted in the Autumn term because there's the new intake of students to sort out and he has to order all sorts of instrument stuff and it never comes in on time and on top of *that* he has to sort out the Christmas Concert and music exams and things, and then people like *you* add to it by bothering him."

"We weren't *bothering* him," said Chloe. "We just went to tell him about our theme."

"*And* we were the first!" said Pop.

"He thought it was a great idea," added Lolly.

"Really?" said Tara, looking pleased. "That's good. You didn't tell him about you pretending to be him, did you?"

"No!" said Pop. "Of course not. We agreed I shouldn't. I'll need to sort out my costume," she added. "In fact, we *all* will."

"I was thinking about that," said Lolly. "You and I are going to look a bit odd singing our usual sort of duet if we're still dressed up."

"So will I," Tara pointed out. "What about my band? It'll be made up of Snow White's stepmother, two ugly sisters and Jack with his Beanstalk!"

"I suppose..." said Lolly.

"You'll still really rock though," Chloe told Tara. "You

know you will. Your music is strong enough to carry you through, whatever silly clothes you wear. But Beauty singing with Pop in drag as Judge Jim…"

"No problem," said Pop. "If it's not going to work with me still dressed up, I can change. You know how quickly we have to change clothes when we're doing a fashion show, Lolly! We just have to be organized."

"I suppose you could wear stuff that's easy to get on and off," agreed Chloe. "That long green shift dress you have is pretty glamorous and it just goes over your head."

"That would be perfect," agreed Lolly. "I've got one too, so we'd look the same."

"What about your hair though?" Chloe wondered. "You won't have time to comb out plaits or white powder, will you?"

"That could be somethin' of a problem," drawled Pop sagely, just like Judge Jim did when he was sorting things out. The rest of the girls laughed.

"You'll only need to hint at his dreadlocks," Chloe told Pop. "*Everyone* will know who you're supposed to be if you speak like that. Perhaps we could make a few pretend grey dreads to pin in your hair."

"Good idea," said Pop. "That gets over the white talcum powder problem too."

"I know!" said Lolly. "Remember that fashion shoot we did where they put our hair in plaits and then piled them on top of our heads? It looked really good. Maybe we could do something similar."

"You're right," agreed Pop. "If yours was already done, all I would have to do would be to discard the false dreads, fasten up my plaits and we'd look the same."

"And with you both in cool dresses, everyone would soon forget that you'd been Judge Jim a few minutes before," added Chloe. "I could hand you the change of clothes and help with your hair."

"Thanks," grinned Pop. "It'll be a bit frantic, but great fun!"

"I can't wait!" said Chloe.

4 Rehearsal Time

"Did you say you were going to be Cinderella in the concert?" Mr. Player said as Chloe arrived for her one-to-one singing lesson with him a few days later.

"Yes," she said. "Why?"

"Well, I've got the perfect song for you," he told her, looking very pleased. "It's about lost love and hope for the future." He looked at her and smiled. "I should think you're a bit young to have experienced lost love, but I bet you can bring some real emotion to hoping for the future!"

Chloe blushed. "I'll certainly do my best," she told him.

"Good. Here are the lyrics." Mr. Player put a piece of

paper on top of the piano so she could see the words she'd be singing. "Read through them and then I'll play the tune and we'll see what you think."

"I like the words," said Chloe. "They're lovely. Who recorded the song? Would I have heard of them?"

Mr. Player looked rather embarrassed. "Actually, it was me," he admitted. "It did quite well at the time."

"Wow!" said Chloe. "I must tell my mum. She's got all your albums. She'll be able to listen to your version before she hears mine!"

"Well, let's see if you like the tune first," suggested Mr. Player hastily. "If you don't, we can soon choose something else."

But Chloe did like the tune. First, Mr. Player played it how he thought she should sing it and then she coaxed him to play it the way he'd recorded the song in the past.

"There was a fashion then for romantic songs with long, sustained notes," he explained. "But the way I see you doing it is much more bright and boppy. What do you think?"

"I'd like to give it a go," Chloe said enthusiastically. "There's an interesting key change in it and I love key changes in songs."

"Good! Let's go for it then," said Mr. Player. "The key change heralds the change of emotion in the song and I think it's then that you'll really come into your own." He played a few bars and Chloe sang along.

"That's right." He nodded. "Keep a light touch at the beginning. We don't need the sweeping violins I had in my treatment. Now, power away in this bit. Well done!"

"I *really* like it," enthused Chloe, when she came to the end of the song. "And Mum *will* be impressed."

"Good!" Mr. Player laughed. "Well, I'll put this arrangement on a CD for you later and you can have a go at it over the next few days. Now, that's about it for this lesson. Have fun with it."

"I will," said Chloe.

She hurried away from Mr. Player's room and headed towards one of the large practice rooms in the basement of the main building. Pop had booked it for the first rehearsal of their pantomime piece and Chloe didn't want to be late. She arrived to find Marmalade and Charlie tossing a toy cat to and fro over Pop's head, while she tried to sort out a running order for the acts.

"They are being such *pains*!" Pop complained when Chloe joined her. The cat flew past her ear and she ducked. "I'm trying to get things organized here and they're just fooling around."

"People always behave worse when they're bored," said Chloe. "Why don't you give them jobs to do?"

"Okay." Pop sighed. "I expect you're right. Marmalade!" she yelled.

"What?" he yelled back.

"Come here a minute."

Marmalade threw the cat back to Charlie and joined Pop and Chloe.

"Can you get everyone together?" she asked him. "I've made a list of acts and a suggested running order."

"I'm on first!" he said, looking at the list and sounding very pleased.

Charlie tossed the toy cat back at Marmalade and it

hit him on the head. He picked it up and tucked it under his arm without comment. "Come on," he said to everyone. "Let's stop messing about and get started. I've got the running order here."

Chloe and Pop exchanged glances and smiled.

It wasn't long before their theme started to take shape. They began with Marmalade as Dick Whittington. He found the Rockley Park poster and showed it to the rest of the characters, who were supposed to be rehearsing a new pantomime. It only took a couple of sentences from the characters to establish that they all wished they were musical like the Rockley Park students. Then Pop came on as Judge Jim and told them to get back to their rehearsal. Everyone fell about laughing when Pop imitated the teacher, even without dressing up like him.

"It would be funny enough if *Marmalade* played Judge Jim," giggled Chloe. "But he's always fooling around anyway. Pop doing it is hysterical because it's so unexpected!"

Danny wasn't quite so happy when it came to the

wishing part. "We ought to have something to wish on," he complained. "Like Aladdin's lamp."

"We don't have a lamp," Pop told him. "You'll just have to imagine something."

But Chloe had her thinking cap on again. "I expect we could quite easily have a magic mirror," she said. "All we'd need would be something like a door frame with some silvery fabric hanging down instead of a door. We could stand in front of it while we wish and someone could hand our microphone, or guitar – or whatever – through the door as if it were magic."

"That could work," agreed Ed. He struck a dreamy pose and held out his hand. "I wish I had a Fender Stratocaster. It's the guitar I'd most like to own."

Danny had a go. "I wish I had a new Pearl Masters drum kit and could play as well as Taylor Hawkins," he said with feeling.

"Okay, we get the idea!" said Pop. "And it's a great one," she added to Chloe. "Where *do* you get all your brilliant ideas?"

"I don't know," replied Chloe. "I didn't have any to

begin with, but now they pop up all the time."

"Well, keep them coming," said Danny with a smile.

"I'll try!" said Chloe.

They couldn't do much more because it was almost teatime. Afterwards, they would have to go back to their boarding houses and get on with their homework.

"Let's meet again later in the week," suggested Chloe and all the students agreed.

That evening while they were getting ready for bed, Tara paid Chloe a compliment, much to her surprise. But typically of Tara, it was a rather backhanded one. "You're a dark horse, Chloe Tompkins," she said, as Chloe brushed her teeth.

"What do you mean?" asked Chloe.

"Well, I didn't have you down as anything much when I first met you," said Tara. "But you're pretty bright, aren't you, as well as being a good singer?"

Chloe wasn't sure how to reply to this. "I suppose," she muttered, wishing Tara's compliments didn't always sound quite so much like insults.

"That mirror idea is genius," said Lolly, when Chloe went back into the bedroom. "And the boys think it's cool too."

"There's still *one* problem," said Pop, getting into bed. "We need to work out how Lolly, as Beauty, suddenly gets a twin when we do our song. Won't it look a bit odd when I suddenly rush off and change into the other half of Pop 'n' Lolly?"

"Why not use the mirror for that too?" said Chloe.

"How do you mean?" asked Lolly.

"Well, if we pulled the silvery fabric away for when *you* look into the mirror, Pop could be standing there like a reflection," Chloe explained. "You could sing your duet as if you're one person reflected in the mirror."

Pop and Lolly stared at each other. "That is *such* a cool idea," Pop said, in an awed voice. "It would be a lovely end to our part of the show. Some real magic! Brilliant."

"I knew she was clever," said Tara smugly.

"Glad you like it," said Chloe, happily snuggling down to sleep.

5 A Generous Present

At the next rehearsal, Pop and Chloe were explaining Chloe's idea for the finale of their performance when Marmalade and Charlie arrived. They were carrying what looked like a heap of old curtains and seemed very pleased with themselves. But Pop was annoyed that they were late.

"You'll have to ask Danny or someone else to explain Chloe's finale idea later," she said impatiently. "There's no time now." She stared as the two boys dropped their bundles on the floor and smirked at each other. "What's all that for?" she asked, when it became obvious that they weren't going to volunteer any information.

"Thanks to my uncle, Charlie and I will be changing our characters," Marmalade announced, with a broad grin.

"What?"

It wasn't just Pop who looked surprised.

"You can't do that!" Chloe told them. "We've all agreed and Pop has worked out the links between acts. Why do you want to change now?"

Marmalade grinned even harder and Charlie laughed.

"Wait until you see what Uncle Bob sent me!" Marmalade told Pop, ignoring Chloe's concerns. "It's so cool that it's *bound* to win us the prize!" He bent down and started to sort out the fabric on the floor.

Pop folded her arms and sighed.

"Can't you leave that?" she begged him. "We need to..."

She trailed off and stared at Charlie. He was putting on an enormous pair of spotted pyjama trousers while Marmalade uncovered a large horse's head attached to more spotty fabric. People started laughing as they watched what the boys were doing.

"It's a pantomime horse!" exclaimed Chloe, as Marmalade stepped into the front feet and put the head on. She went to help the boys arrange the fabric so that when Charlie bent over and held onto Marmalade's waist, the boys became a perfect pantomime horse.

"It's brilliant!" Lolly laughed as the boys tried moving in their costume. It wasn't easy coordinating their movements.

"Only Marmalade would have an uncle who owned a pantomime horse!" said Tara as the boys shambled about, tripping over their own feet and barging into people by mistake.

The rehearsal was in uproar, but even Pop didn't mind. The pantomime horse was so funny that no one could have kept a straight face!

"Do you like it?" Marmalade asked, once they'd stopped fooling around and he'd taken the head off.

"Of course I do!" Pop laughed. "It's great! I don't know how you're going to perform in it though."

"Don't worry. We'll think of something," Marmalade

assured her. "Perhaps I'll work out a dance for the horse with Jack as my owner. Do you fancy doing something like that?" he asked Jack, a slightly built boy who was also a talented dancer.

Jack nodded enthusiastically. "Sounds good," he agreed. "Maybe we could do a short dance without the costume, but with some clip-cloppy music and then link it with a few movements when you're actually in the pantomime horse outfit."

"That could be cool!" agreed Marmalade.

"What about me?" asked Charlie, backing away from Marmalade and emerging totally dishevelled from his half of the costume.

"Well, we don't want you to take the horse apart onstage," said Pop decisively. "Look at you! It would ruin the effect!"

"I could make Charlie's wish for him," offered Jack. "I could say something like 'I bet the horse wishes he could play drums like Charlie Owen'."

"That's it!" agreed Chloe. "And then you could back the horse half offstage so it still looks as if it's complete, while Charlie gets out and goes to play his piece."

"Sounds fair enough," said Charlie.

"Excellent!" said Pop. "That's settled then."

"You're not going to make my end of the horse dance, are you?" asked Charlie. "Because I wouldn't be any good, you know. I hate dancing."

"That's okay," said Marmalade. "It'll be even funnier if the front of the horse dances beautifully, while the back end is useless."

"Thanks a bunch!" Charlie complained, with a laugh.

It was obvious they weren't going to get any more work done today. Lots of people wanted to try on the costume and Chloe could see that it would be impossible to get anyone to concentrate properly from now on.

"Never mind," she told Pop. "We can have another rehearsal when people have got more used to having a pantomime horse in the concert. And it *will* be brilliant."

"Yes," agreed Pop. "And I can alter some of the links to include the horse."

"I'll give you a hand, if you like," offered Chloe.

"Me too," agreed Lolly. "We'll soon get it done if we work together. Then we can give everyone their new lines at the next rehearsal."

"Thanks," said Pop gratefully. "Let's go and get some tea. I'm exhausted with all that laughing!"

As they went into the dining room, an older girl was coming out with some friends. "Hi!" she said to Chloe. "How's it going?"

"Fine, thanks!" said Chloe, feeling pleased. She knew Ayesha slightly from when they had both been in the Rising Stars Concert at the end of last term and it was flattering to be noticed by such a senior student. Chloe smiled and was going to move on, but the girl caught hold of her sleeve.

"There's a rumour going round that someone in your class is going to have a donkey onstage at the concert," she said to Chloe. "Are you doing a nativity scene?"

"No!" said Chloe in surprise, her mind racing. "Not at all. We've got a—"

Pop nudged her in the ribs and she stopped.

"What?" asked the girl curiously.

"Oh...we've got a different idea from that," Chloe finished lamely.

Ayesha looked disappointed. "Well, it's no secret what we're doing," she told Chloe. "My class has chosen to perform all the best Christmas number ones we can find. I think it's a terrible idea, but what can you do?" She shrugged and smiled at Chloe. "I can't wait to see what *you're* going for, if it's a big secret! Good luck!"

She made her way out of the dining room and Chloe watched her go.

"How on earth did that rumour start so quickly?" asked Lolly. "We only just found out about the horse ourselves!"

"I expect Marmalade dropped a few hints to some people before he came to the rehearsal," Chloe laughed. "All you have to do in this place is start a rumour of any kind and it's all round the school in no time!"

6 Horse Trouble!

While rehearsals were still low-key affairs taking place in small side rooms, it was easy to keep most of their ideas quiet. Pop had even hoped to keep the pantomime horse a secret but there was no hiding that. She had tried to get the boys to disguise the costume as they went to and from rehearsals, but it was impossible. The attention was putting *everyone* off.

"You'll have to put on a quick show for everyone," said Pop with a sigh after a rehearsal had been invaded yet again by nosy students pretending they'd arrived at the wrong room by mistake.

"Okay!" agreed Marmalade and Charlie. "Let's put

the word around that we'll be practising outside the main house on the gravel path."

"I'll put up a notice to make it official," said Pop. "We'll agree to show off our pantomime horse if everyone then promises to leave us alone so we can rehearse in peace."

But in the end, a notice wasn't needed. As Chloe and her friends went through the main house, they met the Principal. And she had the solution for them.

"I hear your pantomime horse is causing a few rehearsal problems," Mrs. Sharkey said.

Pop told the Principal the details and she listened carefully.

"There's no reason why you should have to satisfy everyone else's curiosity at this stage," she told them. "It's no one's business but your own. I think some students have forgotten that we are here to be professional in our work. *You* need privacy to get your performance worked out and the rest of them need to concentrate on their own efforts. I'll make an announcement in assembly tomorrow."

"Well!" said Chloe after the Principal was out of earshot. "That should help."

It certainly did. After Mrs. Sharkey's announcement, no one dared to try and spy on rehearsals any more. Unfortunately, the whole thing had made Marmalade and Charlie rather big-headed.

"We're *so* important the Principal has got involved!" said Charlie pompously.

"You're just two boys messing about in a ridiculous costume," Tara told them, rather too accurately for Marmalade's taste.

"We're artists!" he objected. "And this costume is an integral part of my performance."

It was true that he and Jack had worked out a perfect dance. Without the costume on, Marmalade's steps suggested a rather sad, ungainly horse and when he donned the costume it really came to life. Like all the best clowns, Marmalade was giving the horse some real pathos as well as laugh-out-loud moments, and Charlie stumbling along at the back was the perfect foil for Marmalade's grace and balance.

But this wasn't enough for Marmalade and Charlie. During rehearsals, they kept the costume on for as long as possible, staggering about and getting in everyone's way. They were funny, but Chloe could see that Pop, who was impatient at the best of times, was finding the whole thing very frustrating.

"For goodness' sake!" she fumed, when the boys came up behind her and tried to rest the horse's head on her shoulder. "This concert isn't all about *you*! *Everyone* has an equal part to play."

"Sorry," said a muffled voice from inside the head. The horse backed away slowly and did its latest trick, sitting on a nearby chair. Everyone except Pop giggled.

There was a knock on the door and Judge Jim came in. He looked at the horse and smiled. "I heard about this," he said. "Very good! But I hope you're not forgettin' the main point of this concert. We're goin' to be markin' your performances as usual, so there will be Rising Stars points to be won. The music is the main thing. Don't lose sight of that."

"Don't worry," said Pop. "*Most* of us realize that." She gave the horse a hard look and the horse looked away.

Judge Jim laughed. "Well, I really just came to tell you that we aim to start rehearsals in the theatre tomorrow," he said. "I'd like to see a run-through from everyone so I can get some idea of how the whole concert will look. Will that be okay for you? Will you be ready?"

"We'll be ready," said Pop. The horse nodded vigorously but she ignored it.

"It'll just be a quick run-through," Judge Jim said. "We won't be expectin' perfection yet. So if you could all come to the theatre at three o'clock sharp, that would be great."

He patted the horse on its nose and left.

"Well!" said Pop. "Let's go through our links again. And no nonsense from you!" she told the horse sternly. "Stick to the script this time."

"Pop!" said Chloe as a thought suddenly struck her. "Tomorrow, anyone who wants to will be able to see how brilliant the pantomime horse is, but wouldn't it be great if we could still keep your character a secret?"

"It's a run-through of the whole concert," protested Danny. "Judge Jim will want to see how each part works together."

"Yes, I know," agreed Chloe. "But we won't be in costume, so he won't need to realize that Pop will be playing *him*!"

"That's true," mused Pop. "I don't have to pretend to be Judge Jim yet. I can be any old pantomime director. Great idea, Chloe. Yes. Let's save the accent and the dreads for the night of the concert!"

Everyone thought that was a good idea.

"I'm sure our class will win," said Chloe as the girls made their way over to their boarding house. "My song is coming on really well and our theme is so brilliant. Yummy pizza here we come!"

7 A Small Accident

The following afternoon, Chloe hurried to Rockley Park's theatre. She was a bit later than she'd wanted to be because Mr. Player had needed her to go over one line of her song until she got it just right. Now she had the timing spot on and they were both very pleased. All the same, Chloe didn't want to miss her cue at the concert run-through. But it was all right. Her class hadn't started yet because the students before them were overrunning. She crept in quietly and joined Pop and Lolly near the front of the auditorium.

"Hi!" whispered Lolly. "Did you have a good lesson?"

Chloe grinned. "I've nailed that tricky line at last," she replied. "How's this going?"

"Huh!" Pop scowled. "You wouldn't think this lot were older than us. They don't have a clue."

"What's their theme?" asked Chloe, trying to work out what was happening onstage.

"It's Santa Claus," explained Lolly. "And each act is a sort of present. But I'm not sure who the presents are for."

"The audience," said Pop. "But...ah! That's better! He's remembered what to do at last!"

The boy playing Santa Claus was introducing the last act and Chloe waited to see who it would be. It was Callie, a singer who Chloe really admired. "I'm glad I was in time to listen to this," whispered Chloe happily. "She's really good!"

As soon as the last act had finished, Judge Jim climbed up onto the stage to thank the students. "Five minutes over time," he told them. "Not bad. But you'll need to tighten up your links. Okay. Next!"

Pop was already making for the front steps that led up onto the stage.

"Oops!" said Chloe. "That's us. Come on, Lolly!"

A Small Accident

Thanks to Pop's organization, the run-through went very well. Each character was teamed with another person, who handed the instrument or microphone through the pretend mirror when the character made their wish. It worked excellently. The magic mirror, which had been beautifully made for them by Mr. Fallon, the maintenance man, was perfect. When it was Chloe's turn to wish, she said to the mirror, "Oh I *do* wish I could sing like Chloe Tompkins!" as they had rehearsed. Lolly winked at Chloe as she handed her the microphone and Chloe nearly giggled.

But as soon as the backing track flooded out into the theatre, Chloe regained her composure. Her song was word perfect, with the emphasis exactly where she and Mr. Player had worked so hard to get it. There were quite a lot of students watching and they all gave her a round of applause.

Marmalade and Charlie, the only students in costume for the rehearsal, got a great laugh and the linking bit that Jack and Marmalade danced at the beginning got a cheer too. It seemed that the acts and the theme were going to be very popular indeed!

"They look as if they're behaving themselves today," Chloe said to Lolly, as the pantomime horse executed a perfect trot across the stage, without resorting to any extra tricks.

"Thank goodness!" said Lolly. "I don't know what Pop would have said otherwise!"

"Well done!" said Judge Jim, starting up the steps towards them. He was almost at the top when he stumbled and fell onto the stage. There was a second's shocked silence and then Chloe and Danny ran to help him up.

"I'm okay," the teacher told them. "I just missed my footin'." But he looked a bit shaken and was happy to sit down when Pop brought over a chair for him.

"Would you like a drink of water?" asked Chloe anxiously.

Judge Jim smiled at her. "No, thank you," he said. "I'll just sit for a few minutes. I'll be fine."

Danny picked up the dropped clipboard and gave

it to Judge Jim, who looked at it carefully. "Two minutes over time," he told the students. He took a deep breath and everyone waited for him to speak again. "Don't let the time slip any more, will you, Pop?" he said at last.

"No," she assured him. "I won't."

"All right then." Judge Jim closed his eyes. Pop and Chloe exchanged worried glances. The teacher did look very pale and unwell. Chloe was just wondering if they ought to do something, when he opened his eyes again. "Tell you what," he said faintly. "Why don't we break for an early tea now that your class has finished?" He looked out over the auditorium to where the rest of the students were waiting and then back to Chloe. "Could you ask the next group to reconvene here at four-thirty?" he asked her.

"Of course," Chloe said. "I'll tell them."

"Thanks."

Chloe watched as Judge Jim got up and walked slowly offstage. He headed for the door and disappeared.

"Is he all right?" asked Danny.

"I don't know," said Chloe uncertainly.

"It was only a little trip," said Danny. "But he seemed very shaken."

"Well, he's quite old," said Chloe. "And a fall can be more serious, I suppose, when you're old." She and Danny looked at each other.

"I hope he *is* okay," said Danny. "We need him."

"Too right!" said Tara. "He's the best teacher in the school."

It wasn't often that Chloe agreed with Tara, but on this occasion she totally did. "I must tell the next lot to come back later," she muttered and she ran down the steps at the front of the stage to speak to the students who were waiting patiently in the auditorium.

"Did he hurt himself?" asked one of the girls.

"Are you sure he's coming back?" a boy asked.

"He said four-thirty," repeated Chloe. "So I suppose he means to meet you here. Perhaps he went to the staffroom to have a sit-down for a while. I don't know."

The others were waiting for Chloe by the door to the theatre. "We'd better have our tea," said Lolly. "There's nothing else we can do. We'll just have to hope he feels better soon."

"I expect he will," said Danny, but he still looked worried. "I'm going to help decorate the boys' boarding house after tea," he said. "I know it's a bit early for Christmas decorations but Mr. South said we could and at least it will take my mind off Judge Jim."

"We've got some decorations to put up too," said Tara, "but I don't feel very Christmassy either."

"Oh, come on!" said Pop. "Don't be so silly. It'll cheer us up. I expect Judge Jim will be fine after a bit of a rest. After all, he didn't break any bones. He can't be *that* bad."

"Come on, then," said Chloe. "You're right, Pop. Let's get our tea and then decorate. We're not helping by hanging around here."

All the same, Chloe couldn't bear simply to sit around and hope for the best. After tea, she made an excuse and went round by the theatre again. It was well after four-thirty, so if Judge Jim *was* all right, he should be there by now.

When she peeped in, she was pleased to see him chatting to a couple of students onstage and looking more like his old self again.

Chloe ran back along the path to her boarding house, feeling much happier. And when she burst into her room, the boxes of tinsel and streamers quite restored her good mood.

"I've seen Judge Jim!" she called to Pop, Lolly and Tara. "He's fine!"

"Hurray!" yelled Pop. "I thought he would be. Now, let's get some of these decorations up!"

It was great fun transforming their room and when they had stuck up as much tinsel as they could in there, they moved on to the common room. With the help of the rest of the girls in the house, the common room was soon festooned with tinsel, baubles and everything else they'd found in the decorations box. When Mrs. Pinto came in to send them to bed, she was almost speechless.

"Well!" she said after several moments' silent appraisal of their work. "You may all be artists of one kind, but I don't think that includes interior design!"

"Mrs. *Pinto*!" the girls complained and the housemistress laughed.

"It's very festive," she admitted, tucking a stray piece of tinsel behind a picture. "If we don't feel Christmassy *now*, I don't know when we will!"

"*I* feel Christmassy!" Chloe announced, leaping onto her bed a few minutes later. "Everything is coming right, and Judge Jim is fine. Everything is *perfect*!"

"Here's to perfection," echoed Pop happily.

"Perfection!" They all giggled.

8 A Clumsy Horse

Perfection was still on Pop's mind when she woke up.

"You said it last night," she told Chloe as they were getting dressed. "Perfection. I want us to rehearse until we can't improve any more. I'm going to call a rehearsal in the theatre today if I can. The more we can be in the space we'll be performing in, the better!"

The tinsel over Chloe's bed fluttered in a draught and reminded her that it was the beginning of December. "Good idea!" she replied enthusiastically. "After all, it's not long until the concert now!"

The senior students had been hard at work the night before, decorating the main house. It was always their job to dress the Christmas trees in the dining room and the theatre, as well as the huge one that stood in the hall by the stairs. As soon as Chloe and her friends arrived for breakfast, they could see that the seniors had done a great job. The tree in the hall had been hung with twinkling white lights and a host of red and gold baubles. The effect was magical.

"I should think Mrs. Pinto will like that!" said Chloe, remembering the housemistress's opinion of their rather haphazard attempts at decoration.

The dining-room tree was a smaller one, but was beautifully decorated with red bows and gold tinsel.

"I wonder what the tree in the theatre looks like," said Lolly.

They didn't have to wait long to find out, because Pop managed to find a short slot when the theatre wasn't being used by anyone else. "We can squeeze in a rehearsal at lunchtime if we eat quickly," she told the class just before their first lesson was about to start. "Let's meet at one-thirty prompt."

Everyone ate their lunch as quickly as they could and by quarter past one Chloe and her friends were in the theatre, waiting impatiently as a few senior boys finished carrying a stack of large, box-like amps and speakers onto the stage.

"Oh, wow!" said Chloe, catching sight of the tree in the auditorium. It was tall and slender and hung with red baubles and a cascade of golden stars. "Here's something else that's perfect!"

"Come on, you lot. We haven't got time to stand around!" urged Pop. "I want us to run through the bit where the pantomime horse first appears."

They made their way onstage. "Is it okay if we rehearse now?" Pop asked one of the boys moving the heavy amps.

"If you don't mind the amps staying where they are," he told her. "They need shifting a bit further away from the edge of the stage, but if you can work round them for now, it should be all right. We'll go and get our lunch and finish moving them when you're done."

"Thanks!" Pop beckoned Marmalade and Charlie. "I'd like to rehearse your first entrance," she told them. "You're almost there, but it's still not quite slick enough."

"Okay," they agreed.

"When I call you on, remember to miss your cue," she reminded them. "Then you come on in a hurry and skid to a halt just in front of me."

They rehearsed it a couple of times, but Pop got more and more annoyed. The boys were back to their old ways, fooling around and milking the laughs as much as possible.

"It's fine to be funny!" shouted Pop, when Marmalade bumped into her and almost sent her flying. "But knocking me over isn't funny, is it?"

Unfortunately for Pop, Marmalade and Charlie seemed to think it *was* funny. Marmalade nudged her in the ribs with the horse's nose and Pop totally lost her temper.

"You're not taking this *seriously*!" she stormed. "The timings are crucial and you're taking much too long because you're fooling around all the time."

Marmalade poked her in the ribs again and Pop went red in the face. "Stop it!" she yelled, whacking the horse with her clipboard.

Marmalade wasn't hurt at all, protected inside the horse's head. But he reared up like a frightened horse might and tried to turn round. He must have forgotten about the amps on the edge of the stage because he and Charlie careered towards them.

Chloe had tried the horse's head on and knew how restricted Marmalade's vision would be. She could see that he was trying to keep his balance, but it was hopeless. And Charlie as the back end of the horse obviously hadn't a clue what was happening. Being in the costume was a bit like taking part in a three-legged race while you were blindfolded. Once one of them fell, the other was bound to follow!

Chloe watched in dismay as both boys totally lost control. Marmalade was trying to twist away from the stack of amps, but now Charlie was falling onto them and taking Marmalade with him. Their combined weight made the amp on top of the stack wobble. "Watch out!" Chloe yelled as the huge amp started to fall. It made a horrible grinding noise as it slid from the stack. Then it hit the stage with a tremendous thud. But it didn't stop there. To Chloe's horror, the heavy amp slid right over the edge of the stage and into the auditorium. There was a tremendous crash as it hit a drum kit that was waiting to be put in position.

"Danny!" Chloe screamed into the sudden silence. She had noticed her friend down there a few minutes earlier, fiddling with a cymbal. To her relief, his head bobbed up a few metres away from the fallen amp. Thank goodness he had been well out of the way. The same couldn't be said of the drum kit though.

"What have you *done*?" Danny yelled furiously at Marmalade. "You've wrecked the crash cymbal!"

Ed raced down the front stage steps to help. Together, he and Danny lifted the amp off the cymbal. It was badly split and twisted, but the stand seemed to be all right. Meanwhile, Marmalade and Charlie had extricated themselves from the costume and were standing on the stage, their faces ashen.

"I...I'm sorry," said Marmalade. "I shouldn't have been fooling around. But I couldn't see..."

Danny turned from his best friend in disgust and started to take the broken cymbal off the stand.

"It's not your kit though, is it, Danny?" asked Marmalade. "Isn't it a school one?"

"It's still a broken cymbal," Danny told him coldly. "A very expensive one. What a waste of money. Judge Jim will be furious. He's got enough to do without having to order another one in a hurry."

"That's not all," added Ed, sounding very worried. "What about the amp?"

"It should be all right, shouldn't it?" asked Marmalade anxiously. "It looks pretty solid, although it might be scratched I suppose..."

"It's one of the old valve amps," Ed told him. "The sound is brilliant through them, which is why they're always used for concerts. But the valves inside are fragile. They're probably completely smashed."

"So...is it possible to get replacements?" Marmalade asked in a small voice.

"Possible, yes," agreed Ed. "But not easily, and at a price. Judge Jim was talking about it the other day. He loves these old valve amps." Ed put his hand on the fallen amp and looked at Danny. "That's something *else* for Judge Jim to worry about," he said.

Pop stepped forward and took charge.

"You'll have to go and tell him what's happened," she told Charlie and Marmalade. "We can't just wait until he finds out. That would be worse."

"I'll go with you," offered Ed. "I know more about the equipment than you do and I can explain which amp it is. Maybe if he orders the new valves straight away, they might come in time for the concert."

"What if they don't?" asked Pop.

"We'll have to use the newer amps," said Ed. "They're all right, but the sound quality isn't as good."

"Well done, you two," drawled Tara. "You've just made enemies of every musician in the school by wrecking the sound quality at the concert."

"At least we can still *have* a concert," pointed out Lolly kindly. "It's not as if the whole show will have to be called off."

"If only I hadn't been so keen on having the

rehearsal," fretted Pop. "I should have waited until the amps had been moved properly."

"I'm sorry I was messing about," said Marmalade. "Charlie and I shouldn't wind you up so much."

"But it's my fault if I *react* badly," Pop told him.

"Come on," said Marmalade to Charlie. "We'd better go and see Judge Jim now."

"Let's *all* go," suggested Chloe. "It's our class that caused the accident. It wasn't just one person's fault. And the sooner we own up, the better."

"I agree," said Danny. "I'm sure Judge Jim will appreciate the gesture. Come on. If we go now, we'll probably catch him in the Rock Department."

9 Worse and Worse

It was a cold day and there was still frost on the grass as they made their way over to the Rock Department. Everyone was nervous. No one had seen Judge Jim really angry before and they didn't know what to expect. Would he be understanding and pleased that they'd come to own up straight away? Or would he be furious and think up some dreadful punishment for the whole class? Might he even ban them from taking part in the concert? That would be terrible.

Danny and Ed led the way, with Marmalade and Charlie hanging back behind them. The rest of the class followed in a very subdued mood.

Chloe had expected to find Judge Jim in his office,

but as they made their way towards the building they met the teacher coming out. He was carrying a large box and watching his step carefully on the icy path. When he noticed the gaggle of students coming towards him, he looked confused.

"I don't have a class now, do I?" he asked Danny. "I was sure I didn't."

"No," said Danny. "But we've come to see you about something."

"What?" said Judge Jim. "All of you?"

Charlie stepped forward with Marmalade. "There's been a bit of a problem," he said awkwardly. "I mean... a sort of accident."

"It was our fault really but we all decided to come and tell you," added Marmalade.

"Well, what's happened?" asked Judge Jim. He looked around for somewhere to put the box, but there was nowhere convenient. "Nobody's hurt, are they?"

"Oh no," said Charlie. "Nothing like that."

"Well, then," said Judge Jim impatiently. "I haven't got all day." He tried to take hold of the box more securely and glanced at Charlie. "What's the problem?"

"It's the valve amps," Ed put in. "One fell off the stage and smashed a cymbal."

"What?" snapped Judge Jim. He swung round to Ed looking unusually angry and slipped on a patch of ice. Thrown off balance, Judge Jim lost his grip on the box, which fell to the ground. Danny put out a hand to steady the teacher but he was too late. Judge Jim had totally lost his footing on the ice. To the students horror, he fell awkwardly, banging his head on the edge of a paving stone. He lay very still with his leg twisted under him.

At once, Tara pushed past the boys and kneeled by his side. Chloe thought she was going to help him get up, but the teacher still wasn't moving.

"He's unconscious," said Tara. "Fetch Sister!" She peeled off her coat and laid it over the motionless figure. "Hurry!"

Several students raced back to the main building, while Lolly righted the box that Judge Jim had dropped. "Let's take it back into the Rock Department," suggested Pop in a shaky voice.

The rest of the students stayed with the unconscious teacher. Chloe wished she'd done first-aid classes but Tara seemed to know what she was doing.

It seemed to take an age, but it could only have been a few minutes before Sister arrived carrying a blanket. "An ambulance is on its way," she told the students, spreading the blanket over Tara's coat. She asked Tara what had happened and Tara explained.

"Thank you, Tara," Sister said. "You did the right thing. Well done."

"You must be cold, Tara," said Chloe. "Put my jacket on." But Tara shook her head without taking her eyes off Judge Jim.

It wasn't long before the ambulance came.

"I want to go with him," said Tara, when the paramedics had loaded Judge Jim into the vehicle and were closing the doors.

"Don't be silly, dear," said Sister. "Here's your coat. Now, go on to your lessons. There's nothing more you can do here. I must go and see Mrs. Sharkey and let her know what has happened."

"Come on, Tara," said Pop after the ambulance had gone and everyone was beginning to leave. She put a friendly hand on her shoulder, but Tara shook it off.

"I'm going to the main house," Tara told her. "And I'm going to stay outside Sister's door until there's some news."

Chloe looked at Tara's expression. Her face was set and she looked grim, as if she were angry. But Chloe knew it wasn't really anger that made her look like that. Everyone was shocked by what had happened, and worried about Judge Jim, but Chloe realized that Tara might be hit harder than the rest of them. Tara's father and Judge Jim were friends. Maybe because he knew her family so well, Judge Jim was one of the few people at Rockley Park who was able to coax her out of her blackest moods.

Chloe wanted to go up to Tara and sympathize with her. She was rather afraid of being snubbed, but Tara's face was so twisted with unhappiness that Chloe felt she had to do something. "Come on, then," she said to Tara. "I'll come with you. I want to know as soon as there's any news too."

"We'll come as well," agreed the others.

It would soon be time for tea, but Tara even refused to go into the dining room. Instead, she sat at the bottom of the stairs, hunched into her coat. "If Sister or Mrs. Sharkey come past, I can get the latest news from them," she insisted.

Students weren't supposed to take food or drink from the dining room, but when tea was eventually served Chloe and the twins sneaked out with a hot drink and a sandwich for Tara. The news of Judge Jim's accident spread through the dining room and by now there was a large group of students all waiting hopefully in the hall. Just then, Mrs. Pinto arrived from the junior house where she'd been working in her study.

"*What* are you all doing?" she demanded crossly. "You know very well that you're not supposed to eat here, Tara. The stairs aren't for picnics." Then she noticed all their worried faces. "What on earth is wrong?" she asked.

"Judge Jim has had an accident," volunteered Pop. "And we're waiting for news from the hospital."

"Oh, dear," said Mrs. Pinto looking concerned. "But you're not helping by cluttering up the hall, are you?"

"But we want to find out how Judge Jim is," explained Lolly.

"And how exactly will you do that by standing about here?" asked Mrs. Pinto.

"Well, either Sister O'Flannery or Mrs. Sharkey are bound to come downstairs soon," suggested Lolly. "We thought we could ask them."

Mrs. Pinto sighed. "I realize you're all worried," she said. "But the best thing you can do is to carry on as normal. It's time for you to come back to your houses now anyway. I'll phone round and see what I can find out while you all get on with your homework. I'll tell you how he is as soon as I know anything."

It was obvious to Chloe that they weren't going to be allowed to stay in the hall, so it would be better to go with Mrs. Pinto and not argue. But Tara had folded her arms and was looking stubborn.

"I'm *not* leaving," she muttered. "Not until I know he's all right."

Chloe's heart sank. The last thing they needed was a tantrum from Tara. So before she lost her courage, she went up to her and slipped a hand through Tara's folded arms. "Please will you help us make a card for Judge Jim?" she asked. "You know best what he likes."

Tara stiffened and for a moment Chloe thought she was going to pull away. Then she sniffed. "All right," she said grudgingly.

Chloe and Tara went back to the house with everyone else. But no one could concentrate on homework. Most people adopted Chloe's idea and made get-well cards instead. And when Mrs. Pinto came back into the room, nobody bothered to hide what they were doing.

"Oh, that's lovely!" said the housemistress when she saw the card Chloe and Tara were working on. "I'm sure that'll cheer him up."

"Have you found out how he is?" asked Tara.

"Yes," Mrs. Pinto replied, "I have. And you don't need to worry. He's all right."

"Is he back home, then?" asked Tara. "Will he be back at school tomorrow?"

"No," said Mrs. Pinto. "He had a very awkward fall and he's broken his ankle quite badly so they're keeping him in hospital for a few days."

"Oh." Pop looked worried. "But he will be back in time for the concert, won't he?" she asked. "It isn't for a little while."

Mrs. Pinto looked rather troubled. "Well, I don't know," she admitted. "I suppose it depends how he gets on. Sister O'Flannery said he's got concussion and they may want to run a few tests."

"What sort of tests?" demanded Tara.

"I'm sure I don't know, Tara," Mrs. Pinto said, beginning to sound a bit exasperated. "I've told you all I've heard. The main thing is that he's all right and in the best place, but you can't expect him to get better overnight. He's not far off retirement age, you know."

Mrs. Pinto noticed Tara's stricken face and smiled

encouragingly at her. "Don't worry," she said. "I expect you'll be able to send him your cards when we know what ward he's in. And Mrs. Sharkey will probably tell you a bit more in assembly tomorrow."

The girls were very quiet and thoughtful when they went to bed. It was usually good fun being in their room, but tonight no one was in the mood for chatting or having a laugh. All they could think about was Judge Jim.

"I've never thought of him *retiring*," said Lolly quietly. "At least, not any time soon. I sort of assumed he'd still be here when I left. I wonder how old he is?" No one knew, but Mrs. Pinto's words had given them all something else to worry about.

Chloe said what they were all thinking. "What if he's *not* here to organize the concert?"

It was a terrible thought. Rockley Park concerts simply *were* Judge Jim. He had always run them. And it was always Judge Jim everyone went to whenever there was a problem. His unflappable nature and great knowledge gave even the most nervous student confidence.

"And what's the point of having a themed concert if he's not there to judge it?" added Pop. "We're only having themes because of him." She paused. "What if he *never* comes back?"

"Don't *say* that," said Tara in a miserable voice.

"Pop!" scolded Lolly. "Don't be such a drama queen. Don't worry," she added to Tara. "Pop is just being silly. Of course he'll be back. Just go to sleep if you can't say anything sensible," she added to her sister.

Chloe snuggled down and turned off her bedside light. She tried hard to ignore what Pop had said, but she kept seeing poor Judge Jim lying so still on the ground and couldn't stop worrying about him. *I do hope he feels better soon,* she thought. *But what if he really isn't here to organize the concert?*

10 Concert Crisis

The next morning, Chloe and her friends filed into assembly with serious faces. They were all hoping that Mrs. Sharkey would be able to reassure them that Judge Jim was okay and would be back in time to run the concert, but the signs didn't look good. The Principal always looked stern, but today she looked worried as well.

"Some of you might know that Judge Jim Henson had a fall yesterday," she began. "I've heard from the hospital this morning and they tell me he had a comfortable night and will be discharged just before Christmas."

A murmur ran around the theatre as students began to speculate.

"Does that mean before the end of term or not?" whispered Pop to Chloe. "There isn't that long to go."

"Unfortunately, this means he won't be back in time to run the concert," Mrs. Sharkey continued. An audible groan came from the students and Mrs. Sharkey held up her hand for silence. "Mr. Player has kindly offered to step into the breach and will be running things until Judge Jim returns next term," she added. At this, there was a buzz of conversation again.

Tara scowled. "He won't have a clue," she said dismissively. "He's a singing teacher! How often has he had to organize bands?"

"He's really nice," said Chloe in Mr. Player's defence. "And he used to perform a lot himself." But inwardly she did rather agree with Tara. Mr. Player *was* nice. But that didn't mean he was a good organizer. The students knew how easy it was to spend one of his lessons chatting with him instead of getting on with things. He was an excellent teacher for people like

Chloe and Pop and Lolly, who were serious about their singing, but he found large groups difficult to control and he was easily distracted. Having someone like that in charge of the concert could be a disaster!

"I am sure you will *all* want to cooperate with Mr. Player and help him make this concert a great success," said Mrs. Sharkey. "It's at times like these when you have to show your professionalism. Now, more than ever, the staff will want to see a real commitment from you. The best performances will of course be given Rising Stars points as usual, so there is no excuse for slacking. Mr. Player is going to hold a meeting after school in the theatre, so make sure you're not late."

"What about the theme competition?" someone yelled out from the back of the room.

The Principal looked furious. It just wasn't done to shout out in one of her assemblies.

"I will be visiting the hospital this evening," she went on, ignoring the question. "So if anyone wants to send a card to Judge Jim, they can leave it at reception and

I'll be happy to take it with me." Mrs. Sharkey stared hard at the back of the room for a moment. "Euan Peters?" she said. "I'd like to see you in my room, please. Now. That is all. Leave quietly. It's almost time for your first lesson."

Chloe grimaced at Lolly. "Euan's in big trouble," she whispered. "Fancy shouting out in assembly!"

"I said *quietly*!" said the Principal, and Chloe shut up.

Back out in the corridor, the students dispersed to their lessons.

"Well, I'm pleased Judge Jim is okay," said Pop on the way to geography. "But I don't think Mr. Player is a good choice to run the concert. He'll be *hopeless* at it."

"And what *about* the themes?" added Danny, as he and Marmalade caught up with the girls. "It was all Judge Jim's idea to do that. He was going to judge them. It won't seem right to go ahead if he's not there to see the fun."

"I don't want to dress up in that stupid costume now," said Marmalade gloomily. "And neither does Charlie. We damaged that favourite amp of Judge

Jim's and wrecked the cymbal. It's all been a disaster. It was our fault he fell."

"You can't think that!" said Chloe. "He just slipped."

"But I've never seen him so angry before," insisted Marmalade. "And that was our fault. It was when we told him about the broken amp and cymbal that he turned awkwardly and fell. If we hadn't been messing about none of this would have happened."

"Stop feeling so sorry for yourselves," said Tara sharply. "It was an accident. Remember how he tripped onstage the other day? Judge Jim was so stressed and overworked and we *all* gave him things to worry about. I blame the school. He should have been given an assistant *years* ago."

"But he doesn't want one," said Danny. "He told me last term that the school had wanted to take on someone to help him, but he'd turned them down."

"Well, maybe he'll change his mind now," said Lolly. "I hope so."

"I don't think *I* want to do our concert theme any more either," Pop said. "How could I possibly mimic

Judge Jim while he's in hospital? It just wouldn't be right!"

"It's a shame, isn't it?" said Chloe, thinking of the pretend dreads she and Lolly had made for Pop out of some grey wool. They looked brilliant, but nobody would find Pop's character funny with poor Judge Jim in hospital.

The school day dragged and it seemed ages until the end of lessons. Eventually it was time for the concert meeting. Chloe hurried to the theatre along with everyone else. It was a few minutes before Mr. Player arrived and by then lots of students were chattering noisily.

"Quiet, please!" said Mr. Player. "We need to get on."

Everyone quietened down, but then people started firing questions at him and he struggled to keep control.

"Will we abandon our themes now?" one person asked.

"Has the new cymbal come yet?"

"What amps are we using?"

"Can our class have the third slot instead of the second?"

Mr. Player was looking more and more harassed. He didn't have a chance to answer the first question properly before three more were fired at him.

As Chloe listened, her heart sank. She had been so looking forward to this year's Christmas Concert, especially as she'd missed last year's because of problems with her voice. But now everything was going wrong. Judge Jim was out of action and instead of the usual slick event, it looked as if this concert was going to be nothing but disaster and chaos!

11 Mr. Player's Problems

Mr. Player was beginning to look cross. He abandoned the task of answering questions and clapped his hands loudly.

"Be quiet!" he yelled. "QUIET!"

Everyone stopped talking and looked at him.

"There's no point in me trying to help if you won't pay attention," Mr. Player told them. "I know this has been a blow to everyone but we've just got to get on with it. The concert isn't far off, so you must all stay focused. Now..." He took a deep breath and counted off the answers on his fingers.

"One. I don't know about amps, so whoever is involved with them, please get on with it and make sure there *are* amps onstage in the right place at the right time."

"Have the valves been order—?"

Mr. Player waved the question away. "Two. I am not going to change the running order, so you might as well forget about asking." He hesitated for a moment and then his face cleared. "Oh, yes. Three. I haven't a clue about the ordering of instruments, so I don't know if the cymbal has come. But I'm sure you drummers are quite capable of finding a cymbal from somewhere."

"Can we open any parcels that arrive in the Rock Department, then?"

That was Charlie Owen. Mr. Player frowned at him. "Is there a drummer in year twelve?"

"Yes, me," came a voice from the middle of the students.

"Who's that?" Mr. Player asked. "Oh, yes. Carl. Can't you drummers use one of your own cymbals for the concert?"

"Of course," came the calm reply. "You don't need to worry about that."

Mr. Player's Problems

"Thank you," said Mr. Player. "Now, the question of the themes you've chosen for the competition." He looked at the students earnestly.

"I realize that this new direction for the concert was all Judge Jim's idea and that some of you have been wondering if we ought to go back to performing the musical acts like every other concert we've done in the past." He paused, but he still had everyone's attention. "My feeling is that you ought to do what you feel most comfortable with," he told them. "Some of you may want to revert to a straightforward performance, while others may want to carry on with the themes. I can see both sides. So think about it amongst yourselves and let me know later what each class has decided."

Pop rolled her eyes at Chloe. "He needs to make *his* mind up about it," she muttered. "*Someone* needs to direct us, otherwise it's going to be neither one thing nor another."

"So let's have a quick run-through," Mr. Player continued. "I've got Judge Jim's running order here. Let's get this show on the road!"

His words were upbeat, but Chloe could see that poor Mr. Player was struggling without Judge Jim by his side.

"We won't be on for ages, so I'm going to get some fruit from the dining room," said Charlie.

"I'll come with you," said Marmalade. "Coming, Danny?"

"Okay," said Danny. "Don't worry," he said to Pop. "We'll be back in good time. It'll be twenty minutes until we're on."

Pop sighed heavily. "You'd better be," she told him. She watched the boys disappear and then turned to Chloe. "It's going to be a disaster if some people do themed performances and others don't," she said. "The concert will be a total mess. Why couldn't Mr. Player make a proper decision and tell us what *he* wants us to do?"

"Well, I suppose some people are more committed to their themes than others," said Chloe. "Like the class of year tens who are all performing Christmas number ones. It's too late for them to learn new songs now."

"I suppose," Pop agreed reluctantly.

"So what are *we* going to do?" asked Lolly. "Are we going to keep our theme or ditch it?"

"Ditch it," said Pop decisively. "I don't think anyone wants anything more to do with it. Our theme was going to be really funny, but no one feels like laughing now."

Lots of people were muttering about abandoning their themes. It would certainly be easier to concentrate on their musical performances, but Chloe felt very flat. The rehearsal went all right, but although everyone did their best, the whole concert felt somehow joyless.

"There's not much point in having full rehearsals now that so many people are losing the themes," Chloe said to Lolly as they went in for tea afterwards. "We don't need to worry about timing links or anything."

"You're right," agreed Lolly. "What were we all standing around for? We already know the running order. All we have to do is turn up for the concert and perform our individual pieces like we usually do."

"I'm not coming to the next rehearsal," said Tara

morosely as she put a plate of macaroni cheese on her tray. "You're right, Chloe. It's a waste of time."

Chloe regarded her disapprovingly. "I didn't say I wasn't going to turn up," she said. "We've got to support Mr. Player. He's never run a concert before and I'm sure he's doing the best he can."

"If we go, we can give him some advice," Pop suggested.

"Huh!" said Tara.

Even so, Tara *did* appear for the rehearsal the next day, although she stood at the back with her arms folded as if she wasn't expecting to do a lot.

This time, Mr. Player was there already and, to Chloe's surprise, he had a small tape recorder under his arm.

"When the Principal went to see Judge Jim last night, he gave her something for you all," he announced with a smile. "I've got it here."

"What is it?" asked Tara, pushing forward. "How is he?"

The students watched as Mr. Player plugged in the

tape recorder. "It's a message," he told them all. "And, by the way, thanks are due to Mr. Timms, who kindly sorted out how to connect this up to the theatre speakers."

"Well, go on then," muttered Tara anxiously. "Play it."

Mr. Player didn't hear her. He was busy fiddling with the tape recorder and winding back the tape.

"I can't wait to hear what he's got to say," Chloe said to Lolly.

"Ssh!" said Tara, giving her a nudge.

Mr. Player had held his hand up for silence. As everyone watched, he switched on the recorder and Judge Jim's voice filled the room.

"Well, the music on the hospital radio doesn't do it for me," Judge Jim's voice boomed.

The sound quality of the tape wasn't very good, but his voice was unmistakable. Chloe found herself smiling to hear his amused comment.

"And here I am with my ankle in plaster, while you're putting the finishin' touches to the Christmas Concert." There was a pause. "I wanted to be there, but the doctors are being fussy and insistin' I rest. They won't even let me play my guitar in the ward!"

Laughter rippled around the theatre, but quickly stopped as Judge Jim began to speak again. No one wanted to miss anything he said.

"But don't you think that will stop me keepin' my eye on you," he told them. "Don't forget that every concert is filmed for the school archive. And I'm goin' to ask Mrs. Sharkey to make sure I get a copy to watch. I want to see how well you use the themes you've chosen and I want to see if I agree with the staff's choice of winner! Don't let me down now. By the time I get out of this place, I'm goin' to need some *real* entertainment this Christmas!"

Mr. Player switched off the tape recorder and Judge Jim was gone. But Chloe had felt his presence, almost as if he'd been there. And his words had changed everything.

"We've *got* to carry on with our theme now," she said to Pop urgently. "Don't you see? He's depending on us all to carry on as if he'd never had his accident."

"But he won't want us to be the pantomime horse," said Marmalade. "That would just remind him of the damage we've done."

"But the pantomime horse is *funny*," Tara reminded him. "And he wants to be entertained. If you perform well, at least *something* good will come out of your costume."

Chloe looked at Tara with admiration. "Wow," she said. "That's one of the most positive things I've ever heard you say!"

The whole theatre was full of students chattering excitedly. Judge Jim's message had certainly made an impression. Chloe looked at the festive tree, covered in those sparkling gold stars. She could feel herself beginning to get Christmassy again. It had felt wrong to give up on their theme and now she was sure they *should* keep going exactly as they had originally planned.

"We mustn't change a thing!" she told Pop. "We can't call ourselves professionals if we give up at the first hurdle. That's what Judge Jim was saying really, wasn't it?"

"We don't have any choice," agreed Pop. "He knows what all the themes were going to be, so he'll soon notice if we cut anything out. The pantomime horse stays. But for goodness' sake, don't have any more accidents!"

"What about your Judge Jim impression?" asked Lolly. "Are you still going to do that? After all, he didn't know about that, did he?"

"What do you think?" Pop asked.

Everyone looked at each other. No one was quite sure what to say. In the end, it was Tara who made the decision.

"Some students might think it's in bad taste," she said. "But I still think it'll make him laugh – and that's what's important. But make sure you have a bandage on one ankle and use a stick. Otherwise, he'll say you're not being authentic!"

"All right," agreed Pop. "I'll do it for him."

Sister O'Flannery, who as well as taking care of any sick students was also in charge of a mixed collection of costumes that had built up over the years, was kept very busy finding suitable clothes for the students. Pop, Lolly and Chloe didn't need her help, but the school nurse came up with a great cloak to finish off Tara's wicked stepmother outfit. And Marmalade and Charlie climbed carefully back into their costume and practised with a renewed determination.

Time flew by as rehearsals were squeezed into every free moment. The concert was only a couple of days away, but there were other things to think about too. As soon as the show was over, it would be the end of term. Most of the parents would be coming for the performance so they could take their children home afterwards. Chloe started to get excited about seeing her family again. It seemed ages since she'd been home at half-term.

The students were allowed to leave most of their belongings at school over the holidays, but there was still some packing to do and Christmas cards to write to all her school friends. There was so much to get excited about at Christmastime!

12 Concert Day

During the last assembly before the concert, Mrs. Sharkey gave the students an update on Judge Jim's progress. "The doctors are very pleased with the way his ankle is healing," she told them. Then she paused and looked at all the anxious faces below her. "However, I have to warn you that he won't be back with us straight away at the beginning of next term," she added.

There was a gasp of disappointment.

"He has agreed to have complete rest for a couple of months," she told them. "And when he comes back, I hope you will all be as helpful as possible in the Rock Department."

There was a murmur of agreement.

"I'm going to go and see him in hospital," announced Tara as they filed out of assembly.

"Why?" asked Danny. "You heard. He's supposed to have complete rest. How will your visit help?"

"Anyway, you won't be allowed," said Lolly. "And you can't go without permission."

Chloe noticed Tara's expression, twisted with disappointment. But Chloe was sure Lolly was right. Tara would never get permission to visit the teacher. She just hoped Tara wouldn't decide to do anything stupid to get her way.

The day whizzed by, with last-minute things to sort out for the concert, as well as a full day of lessons, and Chloe soon forgot her concern about Tara. But when she nipped back to their room to collect some history homework, she was startled to see Tara putting on her coat and looking very much as if she was about to go somewhere.

"What are you doing?" she asked.

"None of your business!" snapped Tara, managing to look both guilty and defiant at the same time.

"Oh, Tara," said Chloe, realizing what she was up to. "You really *can't* just walk out of school and visit Judge Jim. You'll get into terrible trouble."

"I don't care," said Tara. "I've *got* to see him. They're not telling us the truth about him. He's only broken his ankle, but now we're told he has to rest for two whole months! You know how overworked he is… What if he's decided to pack it all in and retire?"

"But going to see him will only cause more trouble," said Chloe. "And if he's fed up with us because of things like the damaged amp and the cymbal, it'll only make things worse."

"But you don't understand," Tara told Chloe. "I couldn't *bear* it if we came back next term to be told he'd retired. And he might!"

Tara didn't look or sound as if she was in any mood to be reasonable. And Chloe could sympathize with her. It *would* be terrible if Judge Jim wasn't at the school any more. Was it possible? What if Mrs. Sharkey *wasn't* telling them the truth? Maybe he had *already* decided to retire and the Principal was just trying to soften the blow by telling them bit by bit. How could they find out what was going on without asking Judge Jim himself?

"Do you know when visiting hours are?" Chloe asked Tara.

"Of course!" said Tara. "I wouldn't go without finding *that* out! I phoned the hospital from my mobile and they said that visiting time was from three until eight o'clock and that he *was* allowed visitors."

"So there's no *medical* reason why students shouldn't visit him," mused Chloe.

"Exactly!" said Tara, doing up her coat.

"So why don't we make it an *official* visit?" suggested Chloe as a germ of an idea began to grow.

"What do you mean?" asked Tara, pausing at the last button on her coat.

"Well..." Chloe grinned at her roommate. "You know how he told us that he'd need entertaining and that he was sorry to miss the concert?"

"Yes?" Tara was looking impatient.

"Well, what if we took a bit of the concert to him?"

"You mean we should go and perform just for him?"

"And anyone else in hospital who wanted to listen. In fact, *that* would be the way to make *sure* we got permission!" said Chloe.

"Say that we want to go into the hospital to cheer up the patients?" said Tara with sudden understanding and a smile that lit up her face. "That's brilliant. Surely Mrs. Sharkey couldn't say no to such a good idea!"

"And while we're there, we can have a word with Judge Jim and find out what's *really* going on," said Chloe. "I mean," she added in a rush, "probably nothing *is* going on, but we'd be glad if we knew for sure, wouldn't we?"

Tara looked happier than she had for days. "Let's tell the others!" she said, taking her coat off and flinging it on the bed.

"And we can go to ask Mrs. Sharkey just before tea," said Chloe.

"Yes," agreed Tara. She smiled and then looked at Chloe more seriously. "Thank you," she added, to Chloe's great surprise.

✳

Everyone loved Chloe's latest idea and a whole group of them went to put it to Mrs. Sharkey. She agreed that it was a wonderful plan and immediately phoned the hospital to ask if they would like her students to entertain the patients. The reaction from the hospital was very positive.

"The staff are thrilled," the Principal told Chloe. "I don't know why we haven't thought of doing this sort of thing before. The Ward Sister told me that the staff will enjoy it as much as the patients. Well done, Chloe, for coming up with such a public-spirited idea!"

Chloe blushed. She couldn't admit that first of all it had been an idea to keep Tara out of trouble!

"Now, we have to decide the best time for you to go and do this good deed," said Mrs. Sharkey. "Tomorrow is the last day of term and, with the concert as well, it's going to be very busy."

"Could we go straight after the concert?" asked Chloe. "It's not far to the hospital, is it? We could perform for the patients while everyone at school is having a drink after the performances."

"That could work," agreed Mrs. Sharkey. "But I'll need to contact your relatives to get their permission. I don't want a lot of angry parents on my hands wondering where their children have gone!"

"We'll text them too," said Pop. "But you don't need to worry. The parents all natter to each other for ages after the Christmas Concert. They'll hardly notice we've gone."

"Off you go, then," said the Principal. "I'll sort out permission from your parents and find someone to drive you to the hospital."

"Brilliant!" said Lolly, as soon as they were out of Mrs. Sharkey's office. "It's going to be such fun! Well done, Chloe, for thinking of it. "

"Two performances in one day!" said Pop in a very pleased voice. "How cool is that?"

Tara glanced at Chloe and gave her a little smile. Chloe beamed back, her heart singing. Everyone was happy and Christmas was almost here!

Concert Day

✳

The next day, the girls were up early. They stripped their beds for the housekeeper, finished packing and left their bags ready to load into their parents' cars. Because it was concert day, there were no lessons so the students could put the finishing touches to their performances. Tara raced off to the Rock Department, where she was due to run through the song she was going to play with Danny, Ed and Ben. Pop and Lolly went to practise their duet, while Chloe tried to find a quiet corner so she could make sure her song was as perfect as it could possibly be.

She peeped into the rehearsal rooms, but they were all taken. Everywhere she looked there was someone singing or playing an instrument. *I know!* she said to herself as she passed yet another occupied room. *It'll be chilly, but I bet no one is in Judge Jim's secret place!*

On the day Chloe had first come to Rockley Park for her audition, she had got very upset and had found her way to a small courtyard. It wasn't really secret, but was simply overlooked by most people, which was probably why Judge Jim ate his lunchtime sandwich there most days.

Sure enough, when Chloe pushed the door open, the little courtyard was empty. She went over to the old bench and sat down. The sun was too low to reach here at this time of the year and it was cold, but Chloe didn't mind. She sat for a moment remembering the first time she had met Judge Jim Henson.

She had run into the courtyard from a disastrous audition, sure she'd lost her chance of a place at the school. And Judge Jim had found her here in floods of tears. She had never met him before, but he had spent ages calming her down and had even taken her back to Mr. Player to see if he'd give her a second chance.

Chloe owed Judge Jim a lot and was very fond of him, but his fall had brought it home to her just how much every other student loved him too. Perhaps they all had stories they could tell about the way Judge Jim had helped them. And now he'd broken his ankle and needed lots of rest. The more Chloe thought about it, the more she thought Tara might be right. The teacher had already retired from touring with his band. One day, he would certainly want to retire from Rockley Park as well. And that day might be very soon.

Chloe couldn't bear to think about school without Judge Jim, but she knew that more than anything he would want his students to stay focused and be professional. Whatever happened, Chloe knew that he'd want her to give the best performance she possibly could today. She owed him that. They all did. So she stood up and did some breathing exercises. Then she sang the song she'd practised with Mr. Player. Her voice sounded good and she was word perfect.

When she'd finished, it was time to go and watch out for her parents' arrival. They would be there any minute. Chloe couldn't wait to see them. She left the little courtyard and raced into the main hall. Some parents were there already and more cars were streaming up the drive.

"There's your mum's car!" she said to Lolly, joining the twins at the front door.

The sleek Mercedes pulled up with a crunch of gravel, and Mrs. Lowther got out. Chloe watched as the twins raced to greet her. The three of them made an impossibly glamorous trio!

After the Lowthers had gone in for lunch, Chloe spotted her own parents' car coming up the drive. As soon as it stopped, she raced over and opened the door.

"Are we late?" asked her dad. "The traffic was awful."

"No, you're just in time," Chloe told him, giving him a big hug. She hugged her mum as well and then opened the back door to let her little brother out. Ben was reaching his arms up to be lifted out of the car.

"Me too!" he said.

"Wait a minute," she told him, as she struggled to undo his harness. "There you are!"

It was lovely being with her family again, but then Chloe noticed Tara loitering by the door looking wistfully at all the happy reunions. As usual, Tara's parents were too busy to collect their daughter and

Tara would be going home in a taxi. Chloe realized how lucky she was that her family had come to the concert. It wouldn't hurt her to share them a bit. "Come and have lunch with us, Tara," she said. "Then we'll have to go and put our costumes on. It's almost time!"

13 Concert Time

"I *wish* I could sing like Chloe Tompkins!"

The theatre was packed with parents and the concert was in full swing. The pantomime theme was going down well with the audience and the pantomime horse was bringing loads of laughs, but now it was Chloe's turn. She gazed yearningly at the magic mirror and Lolly's hand appeared holding a microphone. Chloe took it and moved to the front of the stage. The music swelled and Chloe began to sing.

She usually sang in jeans and a top, but today Chloe was dressed in Pop's sequin-covered dress and sparkling shoes. They made her feel very special, almost like a princess. Surely Cinderella must have worn a dress like this when she went to the ball!

It was fun dressing up for a change, but Chloe was still totally focused on her performance. She wanted to do her best for her parents, for Mr. Player, who was standing anxiously in the wings with Judge Jim's clipboard, and of course for Judge Jim, who would eventually see the recording of the concert. But Chloe also wanted to do her best for herself. She was serious about making a career as a singer and knew that she would only achieve it if she was totally professional. She gave the song everything and was satisfied as the final notes died away and the applause began. Now she could relax and enjoy the rest of her classmates' performances.

The pantomime horse came on again and gales of laughter swept through the theatre as Charlie's back half stumbled after Marmalade's rather more graceful front half. Marmalade's dance went down well with the audience and Pop's imitation of Judge Jim got lots of amused laughter, though maybe not quite as much as if Judge Jim had been there in person.

There was a bit of a hitch when Tara, Danny, Ed and Ben went to make their wishes. Because they were playing together, they had to wish at the same time. The magic mirror was kept very busy as guitars and drumsticks were handed through, but it was going well until Tara's Rickenbacker bass got caught in the silvery curtain that was the pretend mirror.

"Don't pull!" hissed Lolly from behind the curtain, as she tried to disentangle the bass.

"Hurry up," Tara whispered back. "I can't keep standing here much longer!"

Thank goodness! thought Chloe as the bass came free and Tara rushed to plug it into an amp.

The climax of the theme was Pop and Lolly's duet. Chloe was on hand to help Pop discard her dreadlocks and climb into an identical dress to the one Lolly was wearing.

"Well done!" whispered Chloe as Pop got changed in a flash. Marmalade and Charlie were providing a distraction as the girls put the finishing touches to Pop's hair. Then Pop stood behind the magic mirror.

They had rehearsed it so that the girls would be standing as perfect mirror images of each other. Chloe checked that they were both in place and then reached out and pulled the curtain away, revealing Pop framed in the mirror.

The audience gasped. It had been obvious before that the mirror was simply a bit of silvery fabric hanging in a frame, but now with the fabric gone it really looked as if Lolly were being reflected. The twins sang the first verse of their song as if they were one person and a reflection, but for the second verse, Pop stepped through the mirror and took her twin's hand. They finished the song as Pop 'n' Lolly the famous singing twins. Then Pop stepped back through the frame and became Lolly's reflection once more. The applause was deafening and all the pantomime characters had to come out and take a bow together.

Pop grinned at Chloe as they went offstage again. "Reckon we're in with a good chance of winning that prize!" she said.

"Me too!" said Chloe.

Christmas Stars

But there wasn't time to congratulate each other. Mrs. Jones, the school pianist, had offered to take Chloe and her friends to the hospital. What's more, she was going to take them now, before the Christmas Concert had ended. It meant they would miss seeing the other acts, but it also meant that their parents wouldn't have to wait so long before they could take their children home.

Chloe and the others slipped out of the theatre still in their costumes. As they left, they could hear the strains of a famous festive song following them down the corridor.

"I'm glad I'm missing that theme!" said Danny with a grin. "I've never been a fan of Christmas number ones!"

They bundled into the school minibus with a couple of acoustic guitars. Danny had brought some shakers and a cowbell to add a bit of percussion.

"Here," said Mrs. Jones. "Have a few extra decorations for your costumes." She handed them a box of leftover Christmas bits and pieces.

Concert Time

Chloe and Danny rummaged around and found two red Father Christmas hats. Pop and Lolly unearthed a couple of gold paper crowns and put them on.

"There's not a lot of point you two having hats," Tara told Marmalade and Charlie as they peered into the box.

"Never mind," said Chloe. "Once you're in your costume, I'll hang some tinsel around the horse's neck."

It was only a few minutes' drive to the hospital. It was very warm inside and there were decorations everywhere. The nurses had done their best to make the place feel as festive as possible.

The friends stood awkwardly together while Mrs. Jones went to speak to the lady at reception. A few minutes later, a nurse came up to them wearing a beaming smile.

"If you'd like to follow me," she told them, setting a brisk pace. "We've brought as many patients as we can into the day room to watch you. Everyone is very pleased you've come."

Just outside the day room, Charlie and Marmalade

paused to put on their costume. Chloe waited until Marmalade had the horse's head on properly. She hung a garland of tinsel around its neck and a bauble on each ear. Now the pantomime horse looked Christmassy too!

"Can you see Judge Jim?" she whispered to Tara.

"Yes," replied Tara. "There he is!"

Judge Jim was sitting in a chair with his leg encased in plaster up on a stool. At school, he had always seemed larger than life, but he seemed to have shrunk while he was in hospital. It was odd to see him in pyjamas and a dressing gown too. But when he saw the students, his face lit up and he immediately looked more like his old self.

They all performed their concert pieces and Marmalade and Charlie carefully horsed about. When they'd finished, everyone clapped.

"That was wonderful," said the nurse. "Just right. I wonder... We have a couple of patients who are too sick to move, but I know they would love to hear just one song. Would someone like to sing for them?"

"We will," said Lolly straight away. "Unless you want to, Chloe?"

"No, it's all right. You go ahead," said Chloe. "We'll wait for you."

Some of the patients wanted to speak to the students and so, by the time Pop and Lolly returned, Chloe and the others had only just managed to reach Judge Jim. It was odd, but Chloe felt quite shy seeing him out of his usual surroundings. Tara didn't seem to suffer the same problem though. She went straight up to him.

"Are you all right?" she asked anxiously.

Judge Jim looked at Tara. "Don't you worry, now," he told her. "I'm fine. I may even see you for a couple of days over Christmas."

"Really?" said Tara. She looked thrilled.

"Yeah, well…your father gave me a call and asked if I'd like to stay for a few days once I get out of here. Don't know who told him I'd had a fall."

Chloe noticed Tara trying to look innocent and smiled to herself. Trust Tara to make sure Judge Jim would be looked after. And maybe part of that happy expression was because she knew Judge Jim's visit meant she was going to see a bit more of her parents this holiday.

But Judge Jim was looking at the rest of the students. "I'm very proud of the way you all came here to cheer the patients up," he told them. "Whose idea was it?"

"Chloe's," said Tara straight away.

"It was a joint effort, really," Chloe said, smiling at Tara.

"And how did your concert theme go down with the audience back at school?" he asked.

"They liked it a lot!" said Chloe enthusiastically. "Especially the horse."

"I'm lookin' forward to seeing the recording of the concert," he said. "Mr. Player and I are going to watch it together to decide on the pizza prize winners, so I hope you all did your best."

"We really did!" said Danny. "Everyone worked just as hard as if you'd been there and Pop's dreadlocks were brilliant!"

"I'm glad to hear it," the teacher said. Then he looked

at Pop. "Dreadlocks?" he enquired, but Pop just giggled.

Then Marmalade came up to the side of Judge Jim's chair. He was saying something, but Judge Jim couldn't hear what it was because Marmalade had forgotten to take off the horse's head.

"Can *you* hear what he's saying?" Judge Jim asked Chloe.

"Yes," said Chloe, whose hearing was maybe a bit sharper than the teacher's. "He's apologizing for breaking the cymbal and the valves in the amp." She leaned closer and listened to some more muffled words coming from inside the horse's head. "And please don't retire on account of them."

There was a short silence while everyone waited for Judge Jim's reply. He had raised his eyebrows in surprise. "Well, I hadn't reckoned on a *horse* makin' me retire," he said at last with a smile. "Paperwork maybe! That I could live without, but no, I don't reckon on retirin' just yet."

Chloe realized she'd been holding her breath. She let it out in a long, grateful sigh.

Christmas Stars

"You see," went on Judge Jim, "we all have accidents and break things when we're young. Luckily, the school can afford a new cymbal and we can get hold of new valves for the amp. It's not the end of the world, plus I'll bet you lads will be a bit more careful in the future. And listen to me ramblin' on!" he added. "It's not just young ones who break things. Why, I've just broken my ankle!" He leaned back in his chair and let out a loud laugh, much more like the old Judge Jim they all knew.

"I *have* been workin' too hard," he went on more seriously. "And I've agreed to take a proper break for a few weeks. But don't you worry, I'll be back next year to keep you all on your toes. You can't get rid of me *that* easily!"

"Brilliant!" said Tara.

Something in Tara's voice made Chloe look at her. She grinned back but Chloe could see that her eyes were brimming with tears.

Mrs. Jones came to collect the students and take them back to the school. It was time to say goodbye to Judge Jim, and everyone was speaking at the same time. "Happy Christmas!" "Have a good time!" "Don't eat too much when you get to Tara's!" "Have a good New Year!" Even Marmalade and Charlie emerged from the horse so they could say goodbye properly.

Chloe was looking forward to going home with her family and spending a happy Christmas holiday. There would be presents to wrap, mince pies to make and eat, and the tree to decorate. She was also looking forward to catching up with her friend Jess who went to Chloe's old school. Not only that, but she would be on TV over the holiday! They would be showing the Rising Stars Concert that Chloe had performed in at the end of last term. She couldn't *wait* to watch that with her family.

"Happy Christmas," Chloe said to Judge Jim.

The teacher caught her eye and winked. "Happy Christmas, everyone," he said. "I'll be seein' you all again next year!"

✳ **So you want**
to be a pop star?

✳

Turn the page to read some top tips
on how to make your dreams
✳ come true... ✳

✳ Making it in the music biz ✳

Think you've got tons of talent?
Well, music maestro Judge Jim Henson,
Head of Rock at top talent academy Rockley
Park, has put together his hot tips to help
you become a superstar...

✳ Number One Rule: Be positive!
You've got to believe in yourself.

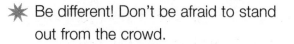 Be active! Join your school choir
or form your own band.

 Be different! Don't be afraid to stand
out from the crowd.

✳ Be determined! Work hard and stay focused.

✳ Be creative! Try writing your own material –
it will say something unique about you.

✳ Be patient! Don't give up if things
don't happen overnight.

 Be ready to seize opportunities
when they come along.

Be versatile! Don't have a one-track mind – try out new things and gain as many skills as you can.

 Be passionate! Don't be afraid to show some emotion in your performance.

Be sure to watch, listen and learn all the time.

Be willing to help others. You'll learn more that way.

Be smart! Don't neglect your schoolwork.

Be cool and don't get big-headed! Everyone needs friends, so don't leave them behind.

Always stay true to yourself.

And finally, and most importantly, enjoy what you do!

  Go for it! It's all up to you now...

Usborne Quicklinks

For links to exciting websites where you can find out more about becoming a pop star and even practise your singing with online karaoke, go to the Usborne Quicklinks Website at www.usborne-quicklinks.com and enter the keywords fame school.

Internet safety

When using the Internet make sure you follow these safety guidelines:

 Ask an adult's permission before using the Internet.

 Never give out personal information, such as your name, address or telephone number.

 If a website asks you to type in your name or e-mail address, check with an adult first.

If you receive an e-mail from someone you don't know, do not reply to it.

Usborne Publishing is not responsible and does not accept liability for the availability or content of any website other than its own, or for any exposure to harmful, offensive, or inaccurate material which may appear on the Web. Usborne Publishing will have no liability for any damage or loss caused by viruses that may be downloaded as a result of browsing the sites it recommends. We recommend that children are supervised while on the Internet.

Look out for more **fabulous**

titles coming soon!

Cindy Jefferies' varied career has included being a Venetian-mask maker and a video DJ. Cindy decided to write *Fame School* after experiencing the ups and downs of her children, who have all been involved in the music business. Her insight into the lives of wannabe pop stars and her own musical background means that Cindy knows how exciting and demanding the quest for fame and fortune can be.

Cindy lives between town and country – with deer and foxes one side of her garden, and shops and buskers a few minutes' walk away from the other. Her ideas come from both sounds and silence.

To find out more about Cindy Jefferies, visit her website: www.cindyjefferies.co.uk